DISNEP's
My Very First Winnie the Pooh™

Eeyore
Has Enough

by Gene Razzo   Illustrated by Josie Yee

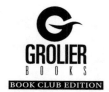

GROLIER
BOOKS
BOOK CLUB EDITION

Printed in the United States of America.

First published by Disney Press, New York, NY
This edition published by Grolier Books, ISBN: 0-7172-6412-2
Grolier Books is a division of Grolier Enterprises, Inc.

It was summer. The Hundred-Acre Wood was filled with bright colors. Green leaves and blue water twinkled in the yellow sunlight.

Eeyore stood by the stream and sighed.

"Ah, me!" said Eeyore. "These colors all look so happy." But Eeyore didn't feel very happy.

The longer Eeyore stared at the colors, the less gloomy he felt. So he decided to play a game of finding colors! If he found enough bright colors, it might cheer him up.

At that very moment,
Tigger bounced out of the bushes
and knocked Eeyore down. It was
very sudden and it scared Eeyore.
"Don't do that, Tigger!" Eeyore shouted.
Eeyore didn't like being scared.

"Whatsa matter, Donkey Boy?" cried Tigger.
"Don'tcha like having some fun?"

"Being scared isn't fun," grumbled Eeyore.

"Hoo-hoo-hoo!" cried Tigger.
"The matter with you is, you
can't take a joke!"

"Joke or no joke," yelled Eeyore,
"I don't like it. You're not my friend.
I've had enough!"

Eeyore turned his back and headed off to his gloomy place. "Tigger should say he's sorry," he mumbled as he went.

Eeyore expected that soon Tigger would come bouncing along to say he was sorry. He settled down to wait. But Tigger did not come.

As he waited, Eeyore saw two chipmunks run past.

"Brown chipmunks," he said. Eeyore suddenly remembered his color game. "Brown sure isn't a very bright color."

"There are brighter colors than brown, and I especially need cheering up right now. I'll keep looking," he decided.

He saw two little o'possums hanging upside-down from a tree branch.

"What color would I call those o'possums?" thought Eeyore. "Hmm, they are a little of this, a little of that, but mostly grayish.
I really want to find
brighter colors."

Eeyore looked around.

Sure enough, right behind him Eeyore spotted two pretty blue birds in a tree.

"Ah, blue is nice," he said. "Still, they are small. It's not enough blue to cheer me up. I'll have to keep looking."

Further on, he passed two yellow caterpillars.

"Mmm," Eeyore murmured, "yellow is bright, but they are even smaller. It's not enough yellow to cheer me up." So on he went.

Leyore walked slowly. Then, right in front of him, he saw two beautiful butterflies.

"Red and yellow butterflies," Eeyore said. "They are very bright and they seem to be happy dancing over a beautiful purple flower. But it's not enough color to make me feel better. I am collecting more and more bright colors but feeling gloomier and gloomier."

"Sssay, sssonny!" whistled Gopher, popping up from one of his holes. "Did I hear that sssomeone'sss gloomy?"

"Oh, hello, Gopher," Eeyore said. "I am playing a game looking for colors to cheer me up. I've found very bright colors but I'm still sad."

"Hmm," said Gopher thoughtfully. "Isss that the only reason why you're upssset?"

"Tigger scared me," Eeyore mumbled. His head drooped. "Tigger hurt my feelings."

"Tigger told me sssomething sssimilar," Gopher answered. "He sssaid you didn't want to be hisss friend anymore. But you know Tigger," chuckled Gopher. "I bet he could even ssscare a heffalump!"

Eeyore said nothing.

"Lisssen, sssonny," Gopher whistled on, "all the bright colorsss in the Hundred-Acre Wood won't cheer you up until you and Tigger are friendsss again."

"He didn't say he was sorry," Eeyore complained.

"No," agreed Gopher, "because you told him he wasn't your friend, and Tigger'sss feelingsss got hurt, too!"

That was hard for Eeyore to imagine. He stared at Gopher.

"Look, I gotta get back to my tunnelsss," said Gopher. "Jussst remember—friendsss forgive each other!" Then he was gone.

GOPHER

*E*eyore wandered along, thinking about what Gopher had said. He kept on walking until he reached Pooh's house. Eeyore peeked in the window. Pooh was home! And Piglet was there, too. Suddenly, Eeyore wanted to tell his friends what had happened that morning. Pooh saw him and welcomed him inside.

"Eeyore!" Pooh exclaimed. "You're just in time! Piglet and I are going to pack up some honey and go out for a picnic on this beautiful day."

"Thank you, Pooh," said Eeyore. "But I don't want to eat anything just now."

"Not eat anything—poor Eeyore! What's wrong?" worried Pooh. "Are you sick?"

"No, I'm not sick." Eeyore sighed a big sigh. "I got angry, and now my tummy hurts. I need to forgive Tigger."

"F-forgive Tigger? What did he do?" asked Piglet.

"He bounced me very suddenly," Eeyore replied sadly. "He knocked me down and scared me. But that's not the worst."

"Not the worst? What else happened?" squeaked Piglet.

"I lost my temper," admitted Eeyore, hanging his head. "I told Tigger he wasn't my friend. And now I feel terrible."

"I know what!" Pooh said. "I'll go and find Tigger for you right now. Then you can forgive him and we can all have a picnic!"

"Well . . . okay, Pooh," said Eeyore.

When Pooh opened his door to go looking for Tigger, there was Tigger just coming up the path to his door! Tigger looked upset, too.

"Tigger!" Pooh called out. "I was just coming to find you this very minute, and here you are!"

"Yeah, here I am, Pooh Boy. Have you seen Eeyore?" Tigger asked. "There's somethin' important I gots ta tell him."

"Well, he's in my house, he's gots ta—er—he's got something important to say, too!" said Pooh. "Come in."

"I'm sorry my bouncing scared you, Eeyore," said Tigger as soon as he walked in.

"I didn't like it, Tigger," Eeyore explained.

"Yeah. I'm sorry, Buddy Boy," admitted Tigger.

"I guess tiggers is scary things, sometimes."

"I forgive you, Tigger," Eeyore said. "Can we be friends again?"

"Hoo-hoo-HOO! 'Course we can!" Tigger cried, happily. "Tiggers is always friends!"

They packed up a lovely picnic. Tigger was so happy to be friends with Eeyore again that he bounced all over the place. Tigger found Roo and brought him to the picnic, too!

Eeyore looked around. He saw a red shirt with his friend Pooh Bear inside it. He saw pink ears. "My little friend Piglet!" Eeyore said. "And Tigger is orange, and Roo is wearing blue, and there's lots of golden yellow honey!"

"With all my good friends and the green Hundred-Acre Wood, I have collected all the colors of the rainbow. And that . . . ," said Eeyore, taking a lick of honey, ". . . is more than enough to cheer me up!"